SECRET-AGENT DAD

by Sarah Willson
illustrated by Idea + Design Works, LLC

SCHOLASTIC INC.
New York Toronto London Auckland Sydney
Mexico City New Delhi Hong Kong Buenos Aires

Based on the TV series *Rugrats*® created by Arlene Klasky, Gabor Csupo, and
Paul Germain as seen on Nickelodeon®

12 11 10 9 8 7 6 5 4 3 2 1   2 3 4 5 6 7 7/0

Printed in the U.S.A.
First Scholastic printing, September 2002

"What do your mommy and daddy do?" Harold asked Susie on their Career Day at school.

"My dad writes *Dummi Bears* cartoon scripts," said Susie. "And my mom's a doctor, a chef, and an airplane pilot!"

"Wow!" said Harold. "And what does *your* daddy do, Angelica?"

"He's a bank robber. Right, Daddy?" asked Angelica.

"Uh . . . no, honey," her father said quickly. "Not a bank *robber*. A *banker*. I'm a banker, princess."

"Daddy, don't you wear anything special to work?" asked Angelica.

"Sure, honey!" he said. "Look! I wore these new penny loafers so I can show the kids how I work with money all day!" Drew said.

"Uh-huh," said Angelica.

"Where's your mom, Angelica?" Susie asked.
"She had to work," Angelica replied.

"Oh, really? What does she do again?" asked Susie.

Angelica watched Susie's mom wearing her chef's hat and rummaging through her doctor's bag. She looked like an undercover agent. That gave Angelica an idea. "My mommy's a . . . she's a *spy!*"

Susie's eyes narrowed in suspicion.

"No way!" said Clark.

"Yup. And my dad's a spy too!" Angelica added.

"Whoops!" said Drew, looking down. "Looks like the penny got lost in my loafer somewhere." He took off his shoe and shook it. "I think I can hear it in there," he muttered to himself.

"See?" said Angelica. "He's calling me on his spy shoe-phone!" She held one of her shoes to her ear.

"The Secretary of Steak says Mommy's on a special a-spyment right now in Tim-Buck-Tooth?"

Everyone gasped.

"Okay, bye, Daddy," Angelica said, turning toward the kids. "Just another day at the office."

"Hmmm," said Susie.

"So, what business are you in?" Drew asked Harold's dad.

"I'm a travel agent," he replied. "And my wife is a real-estate agent."

"Well, not many of us can brag about being double agents!" chuckled Susie's dad.

"Susie," said Harold, "I think I just heard your daddy say he and your mom are double agents too!"

"No, they're not," said Susie.

"Why do you think my daddy's here today?" Angelica said. "To make sure *your* parents don't do anything sneaky."

"My parents are *not* double agents, Angelica. And your parents aren't spies either!" Susie shot back.

"See my dad's glasses? Those are special X-ray glasses," Angelica told the kids. "So he can see in the dark."

Just then the teacher, Ms. Weemer, flicked off the lights to get everyone's attention. There was a crash as Drew tripped over a chair. The lights came back on.

"I thought you said your dad could see in the dark!" accused Susie.

Angelica remembered the pennies in her father's loafers. She ignored Susie. "He also has special cameras in his shoes despised as pennies so he can video-take any funny business."

"We ought to begin!" called Ms. Weemer. "We'll start with Mr. and Mrs. Carmichael. Susie, please join them."

Angelica turned to the rest of the kids. "Being a spy's daughter, I've learned a few things," she whispered. "There's prob'ly a time bomb in Susie's daddy's briefcase. And that cake's frosting is prob'ly poisoned."

The kids' mouths dropped open.

"Oh, and that pilot-wing pin has a tiny spy-mikeyphone in it."

Susie's dad put his briefcase on the table. It ticked loudly. "I brought Dummi Bear alarm clocks!" he said. "Who would like to pass them out?"

"I will, Mr. Carmichael, sir!" Angelica piped up.

The others gasped.

"I know how to dis-mantelpiece a bomb," she whispered.

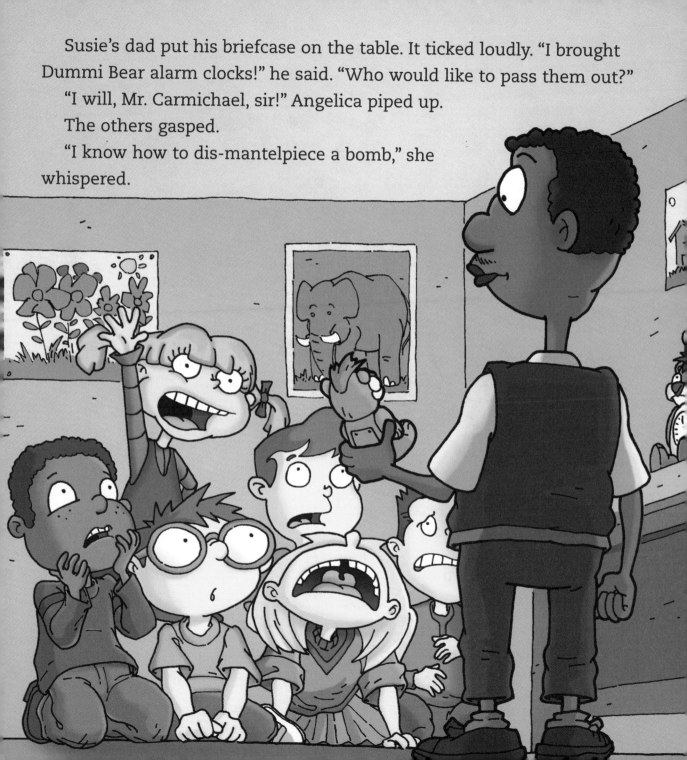

"As some of you know, I'm a professional baker. I made this cake for you," Mrs. Carmichael said. "Who'd like some?"

"I'd love a piece," Angelica called out.

"What about the poisoned frosting?" Clark hissed.

Angelica fished a grimy mint out of her pocket. "I've got a deactivating pill right here," she said, hurrying to get a piece of cake.

"Now I'll show you some of my doctor things," said Susie's mother. She pulled something out of her bag. "Would anyone like me to take their blood pressure?"

"If it isn't the old 'squeeze-it-outta-ya' spy trick," whispered Angelica. "Get that on your arm, you'll say *anything*!"

The kids scrambled back in terror.

Susie's mom looked bewildered. "Well, um . . . who wants pilot wings?"

Angelica's hand shot up. "I know how to get the mikeyphones out of them," she said to the other kids. She rushed to the front.

"Angelica!" exclaimed Susie.

"Dear me, I can't imagine what's gotten into all of you!" said Ms. Weemer. "Angelica seems to be the only one showing enthusiasm."

Angelica beamed.

"Well, now Angelica's father is going to talk to us about"—she stifled a yawn—"about banking. Mr. Pickles?"

"Um," Drew began, "I'm a banker." He pulled off his shoe and pointed at the penny in it. "I work with money, as you can see!"

"Wow!" said the kids.

Drew seemed pleased. "Yes, banking can be quite an interesting job."

Several kids scrambled to their feet, waving notebooks for Drew to sign.

"Gee," said Drew.

"Angelica!" yelled Susie.

"Recess!" croaked Ms. Weemer.

Drew's cell phone rang.

"That's my mommy calling from Tim-Buck-Tooth," said Angelica.

Drew hung up. "Great news, honey!" he said to Angelica. "Mommy's meeting got cancelled. She'll be right over!"

"Uh-oh," muttered Angelica.

"That proves it. Your mom was never *in* Tim-Buck-Tooth," said Susie.

Angelica shrugged. "Is it my fault everyone's so gulpable?" she asked.

"You better tell the kids my parents aren't double agents," Susie said. "Or I'll tell them you lied!"

"Okay, Carmichael. I'll tell them, but you better keep your mouth shut!" said Angelica.

"False alarm clock, everyone! Susie's mom and dad aren't double agents after all. And my parents just quit their spy jobs too," Angelica told the kids.

Just then Drew walked over. "Hi, princess!" Before she could answer, his cell phone rang again. "Oh sorry, sweetie. I'll just be a minute," he said. "I have some more top-secret business to attend to," he added with a wink.

Harold nudged Angelica. "See?" he said. "A-course you're not going to admit that your daddy's a spy! Don't expect us to fall for that."

"Huh?" said Angelica. Then she started to smile.

"Angelica!" Susie yelled, but for once Angelica had nothing to say.